Seth and the Strangers

Jenny Nimmo

Illustrated by Peter Melnyczuk

mammoth

C7078085 99

First published in Great Britain in 1997 by Mammoth
an imprint of Reed International Books Ltd
Michelin House, 81 Fulham Road, London SW3 6RB
and Auckland, Melbourne, Singapore and Toronto

ISBN 0 7497 2884 1

10 9 8 7 6 5 4 3 2 1

A CIP catalogue record for this book is
available from the British Library

Printed in Great Britain by Cox & Wyman Ltd,
Reading, Berkshire

For Daniel and Callum
J.N.

For Kristopher
P.M.

One

WHEN THE CLOUD appeared like a dark stain in the east, a man with a banner walked down Gideon Grove, proclaiming that the end of the world was nigh. Some people believed him.

Weathermen consulted their charts, baffled by something they hadn't been able to predict. Scientists, studying the cloud from lofty windows, told their students it was a result of global warming.

Seth thought it looked like a mighty trap. And when the cloud rained tiny whirling shapes on to the hills, Seth knew that they were not butterflies or leaves or even falling stars. Seth knew that each spinning silver disc carried something extraordinary, something that no one on earth had ever encountered.

As soon as they touched the ground their light was extinguished and he could feel a collective sigh, stroking his face like a breeze.

'It's just as if a giant has dropped his silver,' Anne-Marie remarked, 'and it's falling through the cloud. What d'you think, Seth?'

Seth didn't reply immediately. They were working in the garden at the back of the house; Anne-Marie collecting the last of the beans, Seth turning the soil, ready for winter cabbage.

'I think they're lost,' he said almost to himself.

'Who's lost?' asked Anne-Marie.

'I dunno exactly.'

'Oh, Seth, you're not going all psychic again, are you?'

'I've told you I'm not psychic,' Seth said irritably. 'I just know things, sometimes, before they reach other people.'

'I don't like it out here,' said Anne-Marie. 'I'm going in to see Mum.'

Seth watched her running towards the door, her fair hair dripping over her shoulders, the beans clutched under one skinny arm. He was beginning to think of Anne-Marie as a sister, though they weren't related at all. 'Mum' was Mrs Rattle and she wasn't Anne-Marie's real mother nor was she Seth's. After six years of marriage to Mr Rattle, Mrs Rattle thought she'd never have children of her own so she decided to foster. Mr Rattle liked the idea, and now there were four children in the house at the end of Gideon Grove. Four children with unhappy histories, who were mothered and spoiled and loved in a way they had never known before.

Seth couldn't quite get used to it. He'd been with the Rattles for three years, ever since he was seven, and he still ran away. Mrs Rattle had been so hurt after his second flight. 'Aren't you happy with us, Seth?' she had asked.

And Seth had tried to explain that running away had become a habit. He had just found himself opening the door and running, without a reason or a destination, because it had been the only thing to do when Bill Blainey, his stepfather, started beating him.

'But we don't beat you,' Mr Rattle said.

'We'll never beat you,' Mrs Rattle added.

Seth had carried this news around with him for a whole day. He had repeated it to himself at night, over and over. 'I don't have to run away, ever again.' But the lonely, inexplicable flights had continued. And, while Seth ran, his mind would replay all the scenes of his past. He saw houses and streets in vivid detail; he saw words on a page, maps in an atlas, and every line on the face of the man who had beaten him.

Mr Rattle told him he was a lucky boy to have a photographic memory. Seth wondered why. His memory had never brought him luck, except in school tests when his accurate diagrams drew gasps of admiration. Seth would willingly have sacrificed his gift to escape the pictures of the cruel face that haunted him.

The cloud that was now darkening the sky reminded Seth of his last stormy hours with Bill Blainey, before a neighbour rescued him. The weather had been thundery and almost drowned his cries for help. Seth was told that he'd never have to see Bill again. But he couldn't believe it. Sometimes he thought he would only feel safe on another planet.

An icy wind swept through the garden and Seth dug his fork into the earth. 'I've had it out here,' he said to himself and began to run down the path.

Their house, the last in the row, backed on to the moor that swept damp and dangerous towards the hills, the hills where shining discs had fallen into the bracken only moments before. What were they?

When he walked through the back door Seth suddenly felt breathless. The change in the air pressure was far more dramatic than usual. He told himself that it was only to be expected. It was a chilly afternoon and the warmth of the crowded house had taken him by surprise. And then something touched him. From the crown of his head, right down to his heels, tiny invisible fingers seemed to brush against him.

Two

IN THE KITCHEN, Mrs Rattle sang through clouds of steam. Saucepans bounced on the cooker, their lids clanking an accompaniment to Mrs Rattle's soprano. She always cooked at a furious pace, but the results were always surprisingly delicious. 'Full-steam ahead, Mrs R,' Mr Rattle would tease when he came in from work, spinning his postman's hat at a hook in the hall.

'Take Bingo for a walk, will you, Seth?' said Mrs Rattle. 'He's putting me off my cooking.'

Bingo was a dog with a mysterious past and too much hair. He'd arrived on the Rattles' doorstep one morning, his coarse brown coat matted with concrete. He seemed convinced that he had come to the right house, which he had, of course, for the Rattles never turned any living thing away.

Ever since that day Bingo had been a happy, ready-for-anything type of dog, but now the dark eyes that peaked through his untidy curtain of hair looked curiously troubled.

'He's scared,' said Anne-Marie. 'Look, he's gone all jittery.'

'I think aliens are on the way,' piped six-year-old Hannah. She had been with the Rattles since she was a baby and she was the only child in the house who didn't have nightmares.

'Get away!' Mrs Rattle chuckled. 'Aliens, indeed. Don't you touch any more muffins, girls. There'll be none left for Joel when he comes home from swimming. As for Bingo, he's just lazy.'

'He knows something, mark my words,' said Hannah solemnly.

Seth noticed that Bingo was watching the passage anxiously, and yet there was nothing there. He decided to meet Joel on his way home. Joel was four years older than Seth and knew all about the stars. He had his own telescope and Seth had watched him make a programme for the computer. Now he could show you how the night sky changed in all the different seasons.

Seth fetched Bingo's lead from the hall and swung it temptingly over the dog's basket. Bingo whimpered nervously.

'Come on, Bingo,' sang effervescent

Mrs Rattle. 'You need exercise.'

'I think he wants to go,' said Seth, 'but he's afraid to leave his basket.'

'Perhaps it's something to do with the cloud,' said Anne-Marie.

'Or something that came with it,' added Seth.

'What are we talking about here?' asked Mrs Rattle.

'I don't know, Mum,' admitted Seth.

'Maybe Mr Moon's got the answer,' Mrs Rattle suggested with a smile. 'Listen to him, ranting away. Poor Margaret Moon. He won't be parted from that banner, even to go to the bathroom.'

The children often wondered if Mr Moon was mad, but the doctors had declared him to be as sane as anyone.

'He's just out of work and lonely,' Mr Rattle said. 'Maybe I'd act crazy if I couldn't see the road ahead.' Perhaps Mr Moon knew things that no one understood.

'Come on Bingo, let's go see Mr Moon,' said Seth, clipping the lead to

Bingo's collar. Bingo whimpered.

'See, he's frightened,' said Hannah. 'Don't make him go, Seth.'

Bingo gave a brave bark and leapt out of his basket. Then he ran into the passage, dragging the lead, until he reached the front door where he crouched down, glancing fearfully behind him.

Seth picked up the lead and opened the door. Mr Moon stood by the gate, staring in at him. 'Are you ready for Judgement Day?' he boomed, fixing Seth with a bleak, dead-fish eye. And he pointed to the cloud that was now rolling right over them, low and inky black.

'I don't think it's the end of the world, Mr Moon,' said Seth. 'It's just a cloud, a bit thicker than usual. But did you see what fell through it? Shiny things, like coins.'

'Huh! I saw them,' snorted Mr Moon, craning back to gaze at the sky, and when Bingo whined he muttered, 'The dog knows.'

'But do you know, Mr Moon?' Seth persisted.

'Something unnatural,' muttered Mr Moon. 'Creatures know more than we do. We've lost the feel for things.' He tapped his head. 'It's all gone.'

'Well I'm going to meet my brother,' said Seth. '*He* knows things. He's got a telescope.'

'Take care, lad!' warned Mr Moon. 'It's not safe to be out.'

'OK.' Seth brushed past the big man and began to walk down Gideon Grove. Lights were popping on in all the houses as people struggled to make tea in the early dusk. It was five o'clock on a September afternoon and there should have been several hours of daylight left.

As he paced the deserted street, Seth heard footsteps following him. He knew they were only imaginary footsteps from the past. He knew that when he ran the footsteps would also run. And it didn't help to know that when he looked behind him there would be no one there, except Mr Moon and his banner. Mr Moon wasn't following him. It was Bill Blainey, or the memory of him. Bill and his fists, his boots and his heavy leather belt.

Bingo was a comfort. The dog had perked up considerably since they'd left the house. Seth froze in his tracks, suddenly aware that maybe it was not the cloud that Bingo feared, but something they had left behind them, something hidden in the house.

Three

SETH JERKED BINGO'S lead and began to run. The dog leapt joyfully beside him. They rounded the corner of Gideon Grove and there was Joel, jogging along without a care, his swimming gear under his arm and his school bag crashing against his back.

'Hi! What's up?' he called, as Seth and Bingo tore towards him.

'Have you noticed the cloud?' Seth panted as he drew up in front of Joel.

''Tis a bit dark,' Joel said, 'now that you mention it.'

'Something's happened, Joel.' Seth fell into step beside the older boy, while Bingo manoeuvred safely between them.

'At home?' asked Joel, suddenly alarmed. Gideon Grove was the only place where Joel had ever felt safe. He was the Rattles' first foster-child; a tall, dark-skinned clever boy whom they had loved on sight.

'It's OK. Mum and Dad are all right,' Seth told him. 'But something came into the house, just after the cloud appeared.'

'What sort of something?' asked Joel, raising one eyebrow.

'I can't explain, but Bingo knows.'

'I hope it's not a chemical pong from one of those factories,' said Joel grinning.

'No, you can't smell it or see it or touch it. It's just . . .' Seth struggled for the words. 'It's just there,' he finished lamely.

'Then let's investigate this invisible presence,' said Joel, rolling his eyes in mock alarm.

They ran home together with Bingo leaping anxiously at their heels. Mr Moon had moved on and was now haranguing someone on the other side of the road. As soon as the boys approached their gate Bingo hung back and began a high-pitched whine.

'You see!' said Seth.

'Come on, Bingo,' Joel took the lead. 'What's up then, boy? We're with you.' He half-dragged the reluctant Bingo through the front-door while Seth held it open and then slammed it shut behind the dog. But whatever it was that frightened Bingo didn't seem to threaten anyone else. Mr Rattle was laughing at the telly, Mrs Rattle was still humming in the kitchen and the girls were dancing to wild guitars in their bedroom.

Joel shrugged and asked, 'What is it then, Seth? Nothing's wrong here.'

'Not wrong,' agreed Seth. 'Just different.'

'Is that you, boys?' Mrs Rattle called. 'Tea's ready.'

Seth passed the message on to Mr

Rattle and called upstairs to the girls.

In less than a minute the kitchen table was surrounded. The early darkness seemed to have given everyone an appetite. When Seth sat down he felt Bingo's soft chin on his foot and peered under the cloth. The dog looked up at him imploringly.

'I know,' Seth whispered. 'But I can't *see* anything.'

The kitchen curtains hadn't been drawn and he watched the great cloud reach into the west and smother the last trace of sunlight. Now the darkness was so intense nothing at all could be seen beyond the window.

'I suppose we've got to get used to these clouds,' said Mr Rattle. 'We've mucked up our atmosphere. Isn't that right, Joel?' He always referred environmental subjects to his eldest son.

It was Joel who kept the family up to date with all the latest scientific data.

'This is nothing,' muttered Joel. 'If we don't find a clean energy source soon, the sky's going to look like a battlefield.'

'But we will find one,' said Anne-Marie, with a kind of desperation. 'I know we will. And everything will be beautiful again.'

Hannah began to talk about the animals she would save, but Seth wasn't listening. He was thinking of the sky as a battlefield. It was all very well for the people on earth, with their feet fixed safely to the ground, but what about the others 'out there'. Something had happened to them already. He knew it. He couldn't have said what 'they' were, but he felt their distress round him like an icy current. And Bingo felt it too. Bingo was not afraid for himself, Seth realized. Bingo was afraid for 'them'.

'Penny for them, Seth?' called Mrs Rattle.

'I was just thinking about . . . about what would happen if the cloud stayed here for ever.'

'It won't.' Joel grinned reassuringly.

'Are you sure?' asked Seth. 'Because . . .'

All at once the lights went out.

A concerted rush of sound swept round Seth. The usual exclamations of shock and fright, the 'Ooos' and 'Aaahs' of people thrown off balance, and something unexpected – a sort of whisper that froze Seth's scalp.

'Get the candles, Mum!' Mr Rattle's voice was calm. 'It's just a power-cut, kids.'

Someone knocked a glass over. Hannah screamed and Anne-Marie said, 'Sorry!'

In the silence that followed, Seth felt a
sudden draught that wasn't air rush
towards the door into the passage. He
sensed movement in the hall, a sound so
slight he could have dreamt it. And he
imagined shadows stealing up the stairs.
But whose shadows?

Four

MRS RATTLE STRUCK a match and a candle flickered into life. 'There,' she said, setting the candle in a saucer.

Soon there were three candles on the table and one beside the sink, so they could see to wash and stack the plates.

When tea was over and the boys were carrying candles into the hall, someone rapped on the front door. Joel opened it and found Mrs Moon on the step. 'It's a power-cut, love,' she said. 'A line came down over the moor.'

'Come in! Come in, Margaret,' Mrs Rattle called from the kitchen. 'D'you need candles?'

'Could do with a few,' said Margaret Moon, feeling her way towards the kitchen. 'How long will it last, I wonder. Harry says it's the cloud.'

Joel, squinting into the dark beyond the candlelight, could just make out a bulky shape near the gate. 'Are you coming in, then, Mr Moon?' he asked.

Mr Moon moved closer and swung his banner into view. It was an old trade union banner with a silky fringe. He had covered the original decoration with white paint and now it bore the stark message, THE END OF THE WORLD IS NIGH, in thick black print.

Joel backed away from Mr Moon's awesome prediction, almost treading on Seth who was standing anxiously behind him.

'They're here,' warned Mr Moon. 'Are you ready?'

'Who's here, Mr Moon?' Joel asked.

'He knows,' said Mr Moon, pointing at Seth. 'And so does the dog.'

'OK,' said Joel. 'Mum's got the kettle on. D'you want a cuppa?'

'I'm staying outside,' Mr Moon retreated to the gate. 'I'll watch.'

'Night then.' Joel closed the door. 'Silly old duffer,' he murmured, 'scaring everyone.'

'He can't help it,' Seth told him. 'He

doesn't mean to frighten people. He's got nothing else to do, so he kind of notices things that no one else does.'

'Like you,' Joel gave Seth a friendly shove.

'Like me,' Seth agreed. 'But this time it's not just me. Anne-Marie was with me in the garden when the cloud appeared; she saw something fall out of the sky too. But she went inside.' And he added, almost to himself, 'Perhaps I was the only living thing that they could see, so they followed me. Someone's got to believe me.'

Joel stared hard at Seth. 'I want to believe you, Seth,' he said. 'I'm just waiting for something to happen. Let's play Cluedo. I can't do homework tonight.'

They took their candles into the sitting-room where the girls had already

set up a card game. Hannah was almost
falling asleep so Anne-Marie took her
upstairs to bed. The boys played on
while Mrs Moon and the Rattles
chattered into the night. When Mrs
Rattle came to remind Seth of the time
Joel went upstairs with him. He was

aware of Seth's unsettled state, his quick
stabbing glances into the shadows, his
mysterious fear.

Bingo rushed after the boys but Mrs
Rattle didn't stop him. 'Go on, you great
softie,' she said. 'You can sleep with Seth
tonight. I suppose I'll have to put a
blanket on the freezer if the power
doesn't come on.'

Seth wasn't sure if Bingo was going to
be a comfort after all. The candle
bothered him. He sat and gazed at the
quivering light while Seth undressed and
when he finally blew out the flame, the
dog howled suddenly and jumped on to
the bed.

'All right,' said Seth, 'but don't snore.'

For a while he listened to the
comforting noises below. Mrs Moon
leaving the house. The Rattles locking
up. Mrs Rattle chattering while she piled

blankets on the fridge and freezer, to stop the contents thawing out. The creak of the stairs. Then silence. Or almost silence. From somewhere in the house there came a tiny smothered voice, almost indistinguishable from the familiar whispers of the sleeping house.

Seth listened intently for the sound to come again, trying to catch it between drifts of wind and the distant murmur of late night traffic. And then he fell asleep.

He dreamed that something was tiptoeing over his bed, not Bingo, but a soft coverlet of shapes. Cool, weightless fingers touched his hair, explored his face.

The bulb in his bedside lamp popped on at two a.m. and Seth woke up with a start. Electricity hummed through the house again, and the air in his room shivered as something rushed through it and out of the door.

Bingo leapt after it, barking frantically. Then he sat on the landing, lifted his head and howled, while Seth knelt close and tried to hush him.

Sleepy faces appeared at every door. Mrs Rattle in curlers and a pink nightie

asked, 'What is it, Seth? Another nightmare?'

'No, Mum. It's just Bingo.'

'What disturbed him?'

'Dunno, Mum.'

'Thieves,' said Hannah dramatically.

Mr Rattle rushed downstairs and checked the locks and windows. 'Nothing here,' he called.

'Maybe it was the electricity coming on again,' suggested Seth. 'Quiet, Bingo. Shhhh!'

'Better put him in the kitchen, Seth,' Mr Rattle advised as he trudged upstairs again.

'He's worse on his own,' said Joel.

At last Bingo was quiet, exhausted by his strenuous efforts to alert the family. He allowed Seth to lead him back to bed and everyone called out a weary goodnight.

'What was it, Bingo?' Seth asked as he climbed into bed. 'Was there something in the room, or did I dream it?'

Bingo gazed sorrowfully at Seth, longing to share his secret knowledge. He had never liked keeping things to himself. And this was something outside all his experience, all his understanding.

Five

JOEL WAS UP first next morning. It was Saturday and he was off to the swimming-pool. Joel was a great swimmer, a likely Olympic champion they said. Seth didn't like water. He would rather have been able to swim in the air, high above the ground where no one could catch him. From his window he watched Joel running down Gideon Grove, and wished he could be like him. Joel knew where he was going and just how to get there. He was always busy. Today he would swim until midday, have a snack at the Leisure Centre, and then spend a few hours with his mate, Tom Yardley, in Eastwood Towers. He wouldn't mind if Seth tagged along, but Seth didn't like tagging.

The cloud still sprawled over the town but it seemed less dense. A thin light spilled through it, brightening the autumn gardens. But there was no hint of a breeze. When Mrs Rattle put out the washing, it hung from the line like a row of dead things, limp and damp. The house was quiet and sleepy, so the shock, when it came, was all the more frightening.

The children were all in the kitchen. Hannah, her hands deep in suds was half-playing, half-washing-up. Anne-Marie was drying the crockery and Seth stacking it in the cupboard.

Mrs Rattle came in from the garden, sang out, 'Thanks kids!' and bounced upstairs to change the beds. There was a strange pause in her movements, and an ominous silence hung in the air before they heard a scream followed by the sound of her heavy body hitting the landing floor.

The children rushed upstairs, tripping over treads, clutching at banisters and each other. They found their foster-mother on her back. Her eyes were closed and one arm was entangled in the sheets that lay across her chest, the other flung out beside her.

'Mum! Mum! Mum!' came three desperate cries.

Hannah threw herself over Mrs Rattle's body and clung to her neck. Seth stood watching helplessly while Anne-Marie raised her foster-mother's head on to a rolled towel, carefully eased Hannah away and bathed Mrs Rattle's damp forehead with a cold flannel.

Anne-Marie was always at her best with someone else to care for.

'Oh, my!' Mrs Rattle opened her eyes and gazed up at them. 'What happened?'

'You fell,' squealed Hannah. 'Oh, Mum, Mum!'

'It's all right, love.' Mrs Rattle sat up, blinking. She frowned at the open cupboard and the linen spilling on to the floor.

'Are you ill, Mum?' asked Anne-Marie.

'Did something scare you?' said Seth, following his foster-mother's bemused gaze.

'I don't know, darlings, that's a fact. I went to the cupboard and . . . ' she ran her hand across her mouth. 'Goodness knows . . . something took my breath away, She stood up, her old self again.

'What a silly old fool I am. Anne-Marie, help me get the clean sheets on, there's

a love. Hannah, take the pillowcases.'

'I'll tidy up,' Seth offered.

'While Mrs Rattle and the girls bustled about the bedrooms, Seth gathered up the fallen piles of linen and began to fold them again. He worked slowly, with one eye on the airing-cupboard shelves. On the top shelf, above the stacked winter blankets, something seemed to move in the deep shadow, an invisible and restless fear. Perhaps, confined in the cupboard for a night, it had gathered strength and conveyed itself to Mrs Rattle in a sudden leap of terror. A terror that, for a few seconds, had made her lose her grip on the world.

Bingo came and sat close to Seth while he worked. His round dog-eyes watched the growing piles of folded linen, but every now and then he would glance up at the furthest shelf, his ears

would twitch and his sides heave in
a breathless pant.

Seth kept surprisingly calm. He found he wasn't afraid of the anxious presence above him. In fact he felt a growing determination to protect it. Yet the identity of the presence and the reason for its terrible fear were still a mystery. Seth could only guess that 'it' or 'they' were lost somehow.

'If I could see you,' he whispered, 'I might know what to do.'

Six

LATER THAT AFTERNOON the cloud began to thicken again. When Anne-Marie pressed the video button nothing happened. She tried the light – nothing. The sitting-room had become dark and oppressive.

'It's another power-cut,' wailed Hannah. 'Now I can't see any of my favourite programmes.'

'Whatever's going on?' complained Mrs Rattle, whose chocolate sponge had wilted in the cooling oven. 'It can't be the weather.'

No, Seth thought. It's not the weather. It's 'them'. It's them all the time. They're meddling with the electricity. Maybe they can only escape in the dark. But how are they doing it? He ran up to the airing-cupboard. The door was open just a few inches, so something could have sneaked out. 'Are you there?' he asked. The warm air in the cupboard stirred gently and there was a tiny sound, like the frightened heartbeat of a bird. But nothing could be seen above the piles of linen.

'We're going down to the shops,' Mrs Rattle called up to him. 'D'you want to come, Seth?'

'No,' he said, 'I'll stay.'

'Dad'll be in soon.' Mrs Rattle closed the front door and Seth heard the girls chattering down the road.

He left the cupboard door ajar and went to sit by the window in his room. Mr Moon was parading the street again.

He stopped to talk to someone, a man Seth seemed to recognize. Mr Moon turned and pointed to the Rattles' gate, and the man looked across the road. It was Bill Blainey. Seth ducked back behind the curtain. He began to tremble. The latch on the gate clanged twice. Someone walked up the path. The doorbell chimed and Bingo began to bark.

The bell rang again, on and on and on, while Bingo answered in his gruff this-is-my-house-so-you'd-better-not-try-anything voice. But someone out there was very determined, someone big and yellow-haired with a face like an old prizefighter.

At last the caller gave up and went away. But Seth couldn't move. He stayed where he was, as though turned to stone. So he's found me, he thought. And he'll come back and back until he gets me. Seth considered running, but Bill might still be out there. Hiding. Watching. He heard Mrs Rattle and the girls come in, then Joel. He heard Mr Rattle sing out, 'Cold tea again, is it?'

Anne-Marie called upstairs, 'Seth, where are you? It's teatime.'

Seth dragged himself out of his room. He walked past the cupboard where something hid. Something as frightened as he was. He drifted into the kitchen and found it full of candlelight again.

'Beats me this game someone's playing,' grumbled Mr Rattle. 'We pay our electric on the dot. I'll have something to say when the next bill comes round.'

Seth was glad of the shadows. No one could see his frozen features or the tremble in his hands. He couldn't clearly see the things on the table. His unwanted photographic memory kept dragging up Bill Blainey. And he saw again, just as though it was right in front of him, Bill's broad red palm, and every line etched into it. The heart-line and the life-line, which was very long and curved right round the base of the thumb until it met a deep scar where a dog had bitten him. So he said.

But Mrs Rattle always knew when one of her children was in trouble. 'What is it, Seth?' she asked. 'Why so quiet?'

And Seth suddenly had to blurt it all out. 'It's Bill Blainey,' he said with a shudder. 'He's found me. He was here, just now.'

'When?' said Mrs Rattle. 'No one's

been here.'

'No one but us,' added Hannah.

'When you were all out,' Seth cried. 'He rang the doorbell, on and on. I saw him. He's found me, Mum.'

'That wasn't Bill Blainey, lad.' Mr Rattle laid a comforting hand over Seth's. 'That was Roger from the Bowling Club. He came to let me know one of our dates has been changed. Look, he dropped a note through the letter-box.' He pulled out a crumpled note from his pocket and Seth read the word 'Roger' in a corner.

'I'm sorry,' Seth said.

'Don't fret, lad,' said Mr Rattle. 'He does look a bit like Bill. But that one's gone for ever. You must remember that.'

'Yes,' Seth replied, and looking round at the circle of faces, he found that no one was laughing, no one thought him

foolish. This was a family who knew what
it was to be haunted.

When the table had been cleared they
played cards for a while, then Anne-
Marie promised to read Hannah a story

by candlelight. Seth decided to read something funny, poetry maybe, and went to follow them.

'Seth, stay with us for a while,' urged Mrs Rattle. 'Don't be alone.'

'I'm OK, Mum,' Seth told her firmly. 'I'll take Bingo.'

Seth found a book he knew would make him laugh and began to share the jokes with Bingo. Soon he was smiling, then giggling out loud. Bill Blainey was being buried. Just for now, anyway.

There was a tap on the door and Joel poked his face into the room. His dark eyes were wide, but not mocking this time. 'Seth, there's something you ought to see.' He spoke very softly.

Seth picked up his candle in its blue saucer and followed Joel across the passage. As soon as they were in Joel's room, Joel closed the door, quietly.

'Come over here,' he said. He carried his candle to a telescope on its tripod, just inside the window. Squinting through it, he adjusted it for Seth's height and stood back.

Seth closed one eye and put the other against the cool rim of the telescope. Joel had focused on the hills beyond the moor and Seth expected to see a dark mass, unrelieved by any colour or definition. What he did see was a crowd of tiny, pulsating lights, scattered over the hills like glittery confetti.

'What are they, Joel?'

'You tell me.'

'Some sort of ship, maybe. I think I saw them fall out of the cloud, but then they were bright, now their lights are so small, it's as if . . .'

'As if the passengers had left the ship,' murmured Joel, 'leaving just the sidelights on, until they come back.'

'D'you think anyone else has noticed?'

'Doubt it. Not yet, anyway. It's wild out there. There's no road and they can't be seen from the town. But who were the passengers, Seth? And where are they now?'

I think they're here,' he said.

'Here?' Joel's mouth suddenly dropped open and he stood there looking stupid and terrified as the room was invaded by a tide of whispers. Although the boys couldn't see what made the sound, they could feel the wash of displaced air, and sense the groping shapes that slid to the top of the cupboards, that clambered and slithered over the bed, that leapt and clung, until every piece of furniture, every book and every box lay beneath a swaying crust of *things* that breathed but could not be seen, that were felt but could not be touched. And as the two boys gazed, incredulous and fearful, around the candlelit room, they began to see, but only just, the faint grey outlines of small, soft, faceless creatures.

Seven

'I DIDN'T KNOW they'd be . . . like this,' breathed Seth.

'Nor me,' Joel whispered. 'It must be something to do with the way their bodies react to the light in our atmosphere.'

'Because they're from "out there", aren't they?' asked Seth, needing Joel's confirmation.

'Must be!'

'I think they tried to escape in the dark last night. That's why they tampered with the electricity. But they couldn't find a way. They *want* us to see them, now. They need us.'

In the next room a hairdryer buzzed

on and off, a cassette-player rapped out a brief tune, and then, from Seth's room across the passage, a video-game began with its familiar sequence of notes; it stopped abruptly, just as Joel's computer burst into life.

Anne-Marie appeared in the doorway. A candle-flame shivered behind her cupped hand. 'We fell asleep,' she said, 'Hannah and me, but something woke me. What's happening?'

'We've got visitors,' Joel told her gently. 'I think they're trying to learn about us. They're probably more scared than you are.'

'Who are they?' Anne-Marie peered into Joel's room and a hand flew to her mouth to stifle a scream. 'Oh, *what* are they? What are they going to do?'

'They're not – malicious,' Joel said. 'Not evil.'

'They're lost,' murmured Seth. 'They've got fear oozing out of them, like children who don't know where they are.'

'It was the cloud,' Joel said thoughtfully. 'That's it. They were just cruising around, observing the earth out of a sort of friendly curiosity, not intending to land at all, but they got trapped when the cloud came over, and now they're lost because they can't see the stars and the way home.'

It made perfect sense. But what was to be done? The strangers couldn't stay in Gideon Grove for ever nor, for that matter, could they remain on earth. Seth could already sense their weariness, their failing strength.

'They need a map,' Joel exclaimed. He slipped a disk into the computer and depressed several keys in a fast sequence. The monitor glowed in the dark room as galaxies and constellations winked across the screen.

As each map appeared, Seth held it in his memory, to join the countless diagrams and patterns that had been chalked on classroom blackboards, the notes in history books and the secret routes in the city that he could recall at will.

But the creatures that slipped to the floor and pressed about him were confused. They seemed to recognize the maps, but as soon as the screen showed a different picture, they became agitated. And it was quite clear to Seth that someone would have to take them home; someone whose mind could hold the exact position of every star beyond the cloud.

'It's no use,' he said quietly. 'They can't remember things. They need a navigator.'

Without another word, Seth began to

back very slowly towards the open door. If he turned too quickly, he realized, they would panic. They were already frightened of dying in a strange world.

When he reached the stairs he stepped down carefully, avoiding the faint shapes that floundered beside his feet. Before he opened the front door he looked back. Joel and Anne-Marie were standing at the top of the stairs, their faces mask-like in the candlelight. Bingo sat between them, quiet and untroubled. No need for him to bark now. The fear that had been trapped in the house was leaving.

'How will you know what to do, Seth?' asked Anne-Marie. 'How will you know where to go?'

'I'll know,' he said, and this was true, for as the tiny creatures touched him, he could already see a picture of the distant star they came from. 'Tell Mum

and Dad that I'm not running away, not this time. Promise me! It's important.'

Joel looked doubtful. 'They'll want to know where you've gone.'

'Tell them I'm taking someone home.'

'How will you get back?'

'I'll find a way. I think I need to be "out there" for a while. Perhaps they can teach me to forget Bill Blainey. I just wish I could explain it to Mum and Dad.'

'They do understand things, you know,' said Anne-Marie. 'They try. They're not ordinary parents.'

'They're the best,' Seth murmured.

The sound of laughter came from the kitchen. Mr and Mrs Rattle enjoying their game of cards.

Seth grinned and stepped out into the dark. He could feel the strangers stumbling in their exhaustion, still eager

to be gone, and he had the uncanny
sense that they had come to Gideon
Grove just for him. That they had known
he would be there, waiting to help them.

Mr Moon was standing by the gate
with the banner over his shoulder.

'It's dark out there, son,' he said as
Seth and the strangers passed.

'I know the way,' Seth told him.

Mr Moon laid his banner against the wall and fell into step beside the boy. 'Best not go by yourself,' he said.

They walked to the end of Gideon Grove and crossed the empty road. And then their footsteps were silent as they trod the thick, soft grass that covered the moor.

Eight

HANNAH WOKE UP. She could hear Joel and Anne-Marie whispering in the next room and tiptoed through the dark to join them. They were looking out of the window, and Hannah could see that the distant hills were ablaze with tiny brilliant lights. As she watched, they rose, like bits of spinning silver, higher and higher, until they burst through the cloud above them, and flew towards the stars.

If you enjoyed this
MAMMOTH READ try:

Charlie's Champion Chase

Hazel Townson
Illustrated by *Philippe Dupasquier*

Charlie goes carol-singing to earn
money for Christmas, although he
knows his mother disapproves. On his
way he stumbles upon a burglary and
kidnapping. Charlie finds a vital clue,
but will anyone take him seriously?
The chase is on, but only Charlie
can avert disaster . . .

Another gripping adventure following
the success of *Charlie the Champion Liar*
and *Charlie the Champion Traveller*.